Sophie and the Next-Door MONSTERS

Chris Case

Walker & Company

New York

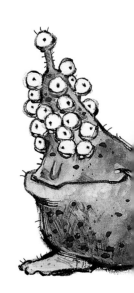

First published in the United States of America in 2008 by Walker Publishing Company, Inc.
Visit Walker & Company's Web site at www.walkeryoungreaders.com

For information about permission to reproduce selections from this book, write to
Permissions, Walker & Company, 175 Fifth Avenue, New York, New York 10010

Library of Congress Cataloging-in-Publication Data
Case, Chris.
Sophie and the next-door monsters / Chris Case.
p.   cm.
Summary: When new neighbors move in next door to Sophie,
she is startled—and afraid—to discover that they are monsters.
ISBN-13: 978-0-8027-9756-8 • ISBN-10: 0-8027-9756-3 (hardcover)
ISBN-13: 978-0-8027-9757-5 • ISBN-10: 0-8027-9757-1 (reinforced)
[1. Monsters—Fiction. 2. Neighbors—Fiction.] I. Title.
PZ7.C26695So 2008   [E]—dc22   2007049133

Typeset in Barbera Fat
Art created with ink, watercolor, and gouache
Book design by Daniel Roode

Printed in China
2 4 6 8 10 9 7 5 3 1 (hardcover)
2 4 6 8 10 9 7 5 3 1 (reinforced)

© Mixed Sources
Product group from well-managed
forests, controlled sources and
recycled wood or fibre
www.fsc.org Cert no. SCS-COC-00927
© 1996 Forest Stewardship Council
FSC

To Mom and Dad

This is Sophie.

She can play a game for four all on her own

and turn her bedroom wall into a circus.

Sophie has a mother and a cat. They don't draw or play games the way that Sophie does, but she likes them anyway.

They are all about to have some unexpected guests.

One day, a moving truck pulled up to the house next door. Sophie watched from the window and saw something that she had never seen before.

"There are monsters moving in!" Sophie exclaimed.
"What if they stuff me in a sack and take me away?"

"No one's going to stuff you anywhere," said
Sophie's mother. "I'm sure that our new neighbors are
very nice."

Sophie's new neighbors had tentacles and pointy teeth.
She didn't care if they were nice, and she said so.

"Well, I am inviting them for a welcome dinner, so you
will have to behave!" said Sophie's mother. "Why don't
you go upstairs and put on your party dress?"

So Sophie went upstairs, but she put on monster protection clothes instead and secretly wished that her dinner guests would just stay home.

KNOCK! KNOCK! KNOCK!
"Sophie!" called her mother.

Sophie came out of her room and
crept downstairs just in time to see . . .

MONSTERS!

Sophie took a good look at them. The father wore a rumpled beach towel tie, and he kept sniffing at the walls. The mother was carrying a sack, but thankfully it was much too small to stuff Sophie into.

"Now what could be in that lumpy monster sack?" Sophie wondered.

Sophie's mother carried her over and set her down
in front of a little blue monster in a dinner jacket.
"Sophie, this is Charlie."

"So who's ready to eat?"

At the table, Charlie changed the color of his tongue to match his napkin.

And he made rude noises until Sophie laughed out loud!

Charlie's mother groaned.

"Sophie," said her mother, "would you and Charlie like to go play in your room?"

Sophie thought about Charlie's tricks and decided that he was safe enough for play. "Okay, Charlie," she said. "Let's go!"

When they got upstairs, Charlie showed Sophie what he could do.

He breathed her toys down from high places,

and he could make up to ten jacket gnomes appear!

He could also wish anything into a potato

(and wish it back again).

Sophie wanted to show Charlie what she could do, too! She made parachutes out of paper towels,

taught Charlie how to make a snake head with his fingers,

and let him try on all of her fancy hats!

Then Sophie showed Charlie her wall circus. Sophie drew a Ferris wheel—and Charlie made it turn and light up! She drew gymnastic bears—and Charlie made them roar and tumble.

She drew food stands—and Charlie made them smell like funnel cakes until both of their stomachs growled.

"Dessert!" called Sophie's mother.

Bump!

Bump!

Bump! Down the stairs came Sophie!

Bump!

Bump!

Bump! Down the stairs came Charlie!

Sophie finally saw what had been in Charlie's mother's sack: cake! Charlie clapped and cheered, and Sophie made some rude noises that were every bit as good as Charlie's.

After more eating and noisemaking, it was time for Sophie's new neighbors to go home. Sophie and Charlie said good night, and Sophie straightened Charlie's father's beach towel tie, smoothing the rumples one by one.

That night, when Sophie went to bed,

she tried Charlie's tongue-changing trick with her pillow.

And she thought that it just might have worked.